Ire.
and the
Baking Contest

Effie Hill

effiehill.com

Light on a Hill Publishing

To Jacob, Avyi and Elijah.

Contents

New Words

Crete	the biggest island in the country of Greece
Crochet	a type of handwork using a hook and yarn
Drachma	Greek money
Festival	a special event where people come together to celebrate something
Greek	a person or thing from Greece
Knead	to punch and fold bread dough until it is no longer sticky
Mandolin	a musical instrument similar to a guitar; it has a short neck and a round body shaped like a pear
Olive	a small, egg-shaped fruit used to eat, to cook, or to make oil
Pigeon	a small bird
Rivals	people who compete against each other in a contest
Sesame seeds	from a small plant; they are used in cooking
Tsoureki	a sweet-tasting bread usually made at Easter
Yaya	the Greek word for "grandmother"
Yeast	a gray powder, made from plants, used to make bread dough rise

Chapter I – Yaya

"Time to come home," Irene's grandmother called.

Irene looked up from her fishing net. She wiped the sweat from her forehead. She was helping Papa mend his nets. It was hard work. It was important work. Most people on the Greek island of Crete were fishermen like Papa.

Irene put down her needle and net. She stood up and leaned over to kiss Papa. She loved the feel of his crinkled, tanned cheek. "Yaya's calling me."

Papa squeezed her hand. "It's time to go home and bake your bread. Tomorrow, Friday, is the Summer Festival."

Irene grinned. "Oh, yes, Papa! And the Junior Baking contest." Her heart raced. "It's my first time to enter a loaf in the contest!"

Papa chuckled. "I know. It will be a special day. It's good that Yaya has come to help. She is a master baker."

Irene nodded. "She has shared many baking secrets with me. But today I must do the baking myself."

"Still, her eyes will guide you. Run along now. Don't keep Yaya waiting."

Yaya stood at the edge of the beach.

Irene waved. "I'm coming, Yaya!" She darted over the wet sand. It oozed up between her toes. The sand turned into pebbles.

Crunch, crunch. Irene liked the sound beneath her feet.

Irene reached Yaya and hugged her. She rested her head against her grandmother for a moment.

Yaya kissed the top of Irene's head. "How is my little pigeon today?"

Irene looked up. Yaya wore a plain black dress with buttons down the front. A gray apron was tied around her waist. "I'm fine. I am so happy you are here," Irene said.

Yaya's green eyes twinkled. "I am glad too." Her wrinkled hand brushed a strand of Irene's curly black hair out of her eyes.

A black scarf with gray flowers covered Yaya's head. Two long, gray braids hid under that scarf. Every morning, Yaya twirled them up and around the top of her head.

They always look like a crown, Irene thought.

She slipped her hand into Yaya's hand. Her skin felt rough.

Yaya's hands were always busy. They picked fruit in the spring. In the summer they made jam. Her hands sowed seeds in the fall. They knitted sweaters in the winter.

And her hands made the best bread on the whole island of Crete.

Maybe in the whole world.

Yaya had taught Irene how to bake bread. Soon everyone would find out if Irene had been a good student.

Yaya and Irene walked hand in hand along the road that led to the village.

"Are you nervous?" Yaya asked. "Tomorrow is the Junior Baking contest."

"A little," Irene said. *A lot*, she added, just to herself.

Yaya nodded. "I was nervous the first time I took part in the contest." She sighed. "That was a very long time ago."

"How many years ago?"

"Too many for you to count."

Irene laughed. "But you won the contest when you were my age."

Yaya lifted Irene's chin and looked into her eyes. "Yes, I did win that first year when I was ten. But now you know all my baking secrets. You will win."

Irene wrinkled her forehead. *I want to make Yaya proud*, she thought. *I must win.*

"Tell me about the time you won, Yaya."

"You have heard that story countless times, little pigeon." She chuckled.

"Please, Yaya," Irene begged. "I never grow tired of it."

Yaya took a deep breath. "I worked all afternoon to knead the bread. I let it rise. Then I kneaded it again and shaped it into a round olive loaf."

"And sprinkled it with sesame seeds," Irene added.

Yaya nodded. "I baked it that evening. The next day I was worried when I took it to the contest. Was my loaf good enough? But—"

"But the judges said they had never tasted a better olive loaf!" Irene burst out, grinning.

"That's right." Yaya smiled back. "You have a good memory."

Irene and Yaya reached the first narrow, village street. They turned right. The cobbled streets looked like yarn winding around the houses.

"Finish the story, Yaya," Irene said. "About your rivals."

"My main rival was Mrs. Lydia. She was a good baker. She took second place."

"Mrs. Lydia is Maria's grandmother."

Yaya nodded. "I hear Maria will be in the contest tomorrow too. She is ten, just like you."

Irene rolled her eyes.

"Maria is a nice girl," Yaya said. "You should get to know her."

Irene shook her head. "Maria is my rival now. I must win first place. She must take second place—just like her grandmother did."

Chapter 2 – Sweet Bread

Yaya frowned at Irene's words. "A contest does not mean that you and Maria cannot be friends."

Irene shrugged. She did not want to think about Yaya's advice. She only wanted to think about the bread she had to bake. And about winning.

Irene and Yaya walked down the first street lined with white houses. Their blue shutters hung wide open. Irene liked to glance through the windows as she walked by. At times children sat on the stone floors and played. Other times, a mother fried fish in the kitchen. Sometimes a family sat around a small table to eat.

At the end of the street Irene and Yaya turned left. Irene's home was seven houses down. She ran ahead and opened the blue front door. "Mama, we're home!"

Irene dashed though the living room. Next she dashed through the dining room, which led to the backyard. She opened the door and ran outside.

To Irene's left, the kitchen also opened up into the backyard. Bright blue shutters framed a big window. To her right, there were two bedrooms with closed blue shutters. A chicken coop stood straight ahead. Next to it, Irene's pet goat was tied to the wire fence.

Irene walked up to Poppy and patted her head. Mama and Papa bought the goat six months ago. "I will name her Poppy," Irene had said. "The red tuft of hair between her horns reminds me of red poppy flowers. And poppies are my favorite flower. I love how they grow wild in fields in the summer."

Irene scratched Poppy's red tuft until she spotted Mama. Her mother sat at a table under the shade of a big blackberry tree. She shelled peas.

Snap! A pea pod split open. Mama's fingers pushed the round, green peas into a bowl.

She looked up. "Tomorrow is your big day. You had better get to work."

Irene's stomach flip-flopped. She wanted to tell Mama how nervous she was, but no words came out.

Mama smiled. "Just do your best."

Irene relaxed. Mama always had a way of knowing what her daughter was thinking. "Yes, mama."

She and Yaya headed to the kitchen.

"You will make the bread," Yaya said. "But I will help with the outdoor oven."

"Good idea," Irene said. "I can't light the firewood myself."

"And the clay oven gets very hot," Yaya added.

Irene cocked her head to one side. "I was thinking of all the types of bread in Crete. Round, long, and square loaves. Some with olives, cheese, or garlic."

"Others with fruit or honey."

"Loaves for New Year and Christmas."

"Loaves for birthdays and for weddings."

Irene licked her lips. "I love to eat them all!"

"Which kind of bread will you make for the contest?" Yaya asked.

Irene took out a large, metal bowl. "I'm going to make a *tsoureki*, even though it's usually made at Easter."

"It is a good choice," Yaya said. "So sweet and full of flavor. The judges will like it. Just remember all I have taught you about baking."

Irene washed her hands. "Do you think my *tsoureki* will be the best bread in the Junior Baking contest?"

Yaya smiled. "I'm *sure* it will be."

Chapter 3 – Baking is Hard Work

Irene put on the yellow apron Yaya had sewn for her. It made her feel very grown up when she wore it. She took out all the things she needed to bake bread. Then she warmed up a cup of milk on the stove and poured it into the large, metal bowl.

"Is the milk just right?" Yaya asked.

"If the milk is too hot, it will kill the yeast," Irene said. "If the milk is too cold, the yeast stays asleep. My bread will not rise." She dribbled a few drops of milk onto her wrist. "It feels a little warmer than my skin. Just right! It is safe to add the yeast."

Yaya smiled.

Yaya is pleased, Irene thought. *I have listened well.* Irene added two teaspoons of yeast to the warm milk. She stirred. "Wake up, yeast. Wake up!"

Soon the milk began to froth. Irene added four cups of flour and one cup of sugar. Then she added a half a cup of melted butter, two eggs, and a pinch of salt.

"Now for the secret to this yummy recipe," Irene said. "A teaspoon of grated orange peel and half a cup of ground-up almonds."

Yaya nodded. "They add a lovely fruity and nutty taste."

Sweet, tasty *tsoureki*. Irene licked her lips. She could almost taste the warm bread.

Irene mixed everything together. Around and around she twirled a wooden spoon. She stopped and took a breath. "My fingers hurt. Stirring is hard work!"

Yaya nodded but did not offer to help. "You can do it," she said.

Soon a stiff ball of dough formed. Irene turned it out onto the kitchen table and sprinkled it with flour. Then she began to knead the dough.

Irene pushed down hard on the dough with the palm of her hands. She folded it and turned it over. Press, push, punch. Over and over again.

She let out a deep breath. "My arms ache!"

Yaya patted Irene's back. "Patience, little pigeon. Just a little more kneading."

Irene pressed her lips together. *I will not give up. I must win!* She kneaded harder.

"The dough no longer sticks to my fingers," Irene said a few minutes later. "That means it's ready."

She put the ball of dough back into the bowl and covered it with a cloth. She looked at the clock. "It's two o'clock. The dough must rise for two hours. The yeast will make it double in size."

"That's right," Yaya said, smiling.

"We'll come back at four o'clock. Then I will form the dough into a *tsoureki* loaf."

"Lemonade while we wait?" Yaya suggested.

Irene wiped her forehead. Baking was hard work. "Good idea!"

Irene and Yaya joined Mama outside. They sipped lemonade and talked about the Summer Festival.

Irene could hardly wait for Friday evening. "Every year so many merchants come to sell all sorts of things. What will you buy?"

"A new apron," Yaya said.

"A new tablecloth," Mama said. "I'm sure Papa will buy new fishing hooks. What about you, Irene?"

Irene sighed. "First place at the Junior Baking contest wins five hundred drachmas. That is enough money for a new pair of earrings."

Second place wins a blue ribbon, Irene thought. *And third place wins a white ribbon.*

She took a deep breath. *But I will not think about blue or white ribbons!*

Chapter 4 – Mr. Oven

Yaya looked at her watch. "Three o'clock. One more hour. We should check on the oven in the meantime."

Irene headed over to the white-washed clay oven. It stood as tall as she did, with straight sides running to the ground. She thought the round top looked like an old man's bald head. The metal door in front was his mouth.

Are you hungry, Mr. Oven? Irene asked silently. She giggled. *Soon I will feed you my sweet, tasty tsoureki.*

Every house in the village had a clay oven in the backyard. Irene thought of Maria. *Is she checking on her oven right now?*

Yaya joined Irene. She pointed to a pile of firewood, tied with string, next to the oven. "Is it a nice, full bundle?"

Irene picked it up. She stretched her arms around it. "It almost fills my arms, Yaya. It is a good-sized bundle."

Yaya rubbed her chin. "I think it will make the oven hot enough. But get extra wood—just in case we need it."

"There are old walnut trees in the field across the street," Irene said eagerly. "Plenty of branches and twigs lying around. They will burn well."

Yaya yawned. "I am tired, little pigeon. You fly to the field to fetch wood. I will close my eyes until you come back."

Irene thought a bit. "I'll find some rope. There are always spare pieces lying around. I will use it tie up my extra bundle of wood."

"Good idea," Yaya said. She headed to Irene's bedroom to take a nap.

Irene picked up a long, thin piece of rope lying next to Poppy. The goat nibbled on the rope in Irene's hand.

"No!" Irene scolded. "No chewing my rope." She yanked it out of Poppy's mouth.

Poppy nibbled on Irene's dress.

"No!" She pulled her dress away. "No chewing on my dress."

Irene headed for the dining room door. "Are you hungry?" she called back. "I will bring you radishes later for dinner. But right now I have an important job to do."

Poppy began to chew on the rope that tied her to the fence.

Irene crossed the street. She gathered long, thin branches from the ground. She piled them neatly next to each other. "I must get enough to keep Mr. Oven very hot," she muttered.

Soon Irene had a big bundle of firewood. She tied it with her rope. Then she reached her arms around it. Her fingers barely touched.

Irene put down the bundle and wiped sweat off her forehead. "A good bundle. Phew! I need to rest."

She stretched her arms and her back. Then she sat down in the shade of a tall walnut tree. Irene spotted a long, straight twig next to her. It looked like Mr. Basil's wooden wand. Her music teacher always used a wand to conduct the school choir.

Mr. Basil waved his wand up and down. He waved it right and left. The children knew when to sing loud or soft. They knew when to sing fast or slow.

Irene picked up the twig. She stood up and stuck out her chest. "Ladies and gentlemen," she announced. "I present to you the winner of the Junior Baking contest. Irene Stavros will lead the school choir today."

Irene bowed, closed her eyes, and hummed a tune. She twirled the twig up and down. She twirled the twig to the left and to the right.

Just like Mr. Basil. But even better.

Clump, clump. Irene heard footsteps behind her. She froze. Who could it be?

She opened her eyes and spun around.

Maria, Irene's bread-baking rival, smiled. "Hello."

Irene felt her cheeks burn. *Oh, no! How long has Maria been watching me?*

Chapter 5 – From Lump to Loaf

Maria looked happy to see Irene. But why was Maria poking around Irene's street?

She pointed to Irene's wood. "Nice bundle. I came to gather firewood too."

That answered Irene's question. She was not happy at all. *I won't speak to her,* she decided. *After all, tomorrow is the contest. And we are . . . rivals.*

Maria twirled a strand of her sandy brown hair. Her brown eyes reminded Irene of melted chocolate. "I hope your baking is going well," Maria said. "Can I help you gather more wood?"

Irene shook her head.

"Were you leading a choir with a twig wand?" Maria asked. "Looked like fun."

Irene's face grew hotter. Maria was making it hard for Irene to act mean.

"I love music," Maria continued. "I play the mandolin. Have you seen one before?"

Irene shrugged.

"It looks kind of like a small guitar," Maria explained. "But rounder. Would you like me to teach you how to play?"

I love music too. That would be great, Irene wanted to say. But she thought about the contest. And how she must win. She didn't answer Maria.

Maria cocked her head. "I was thinking. Maybe sometime we could—"

"You're wasting my time," Irene blurted. "I have to go. Good-bye." She scooped up her bundle of wood, stuck out her chin, and marched off.

Irene glanced back one time. Maria's shoulders were slumped. Maria's hurt eyes stared after her.

Irene's heart sank. *Why was I so mean?* She ran across the street.

Just then she remembered a saying in her village: "An enemy cannot become a friend."

Maria was Irene's enemy. Her rival. *I must beat her tomorrow.*

The wood felt heavy in Irene's arms. She reached home and ran through the house to the backyard. She dropped her new bundle of firewood next to the oven. Then she went back indoors and tiptoed into her bedroom.

Yaya did not open her eyes. "Is that you, Irene?"

Irene lay down next to her grandmother and said nothing.

"Is something wrong, little pigeon?"

Irene chewed her lip. How did Yaya know her heart was troubled? "Maria was in the walnut tree field," she whispered.

Yaya opened her eyes and sat up. "What did she say?"

Irene didn't want to think about Maria's kind words. "Not much."

"What did you say?"

Irene did not want to think about her own unkind words. "Not much."

"Such a nice girl." Yaya swung her legs from the bed and stood up. "You really should get to know her."

Irene got up too. Her stomach hurt. *I was rude to Maria. I wish I could make it up to her—somehow.*

Irene put Maria out of her mind and followed Yaya into the kitchen. Mama was cleaning a large fish for dinner.

Yaya took out white yarn and a crochet hook. She crocheted round covers for her jam jars. Yaya's fingers moved very fast, and Irene made sure the yarn did not get tangled.

Soon it was four o'clock.

"It's been two hours since I kneaded my dough," Irene said. She uncovered the bowl. "Look! The yeast has done its job. The lump of dough is two times as big as before."

Yaya nodded. "It's time to turn the lump into a *tsoureki* loaf."

Irene took a deep breath and punched down the puffy ball of dough. It collapsed like a leaky balloon. "I have a special job to do now," she said. "I have to work carefully."

Yaya watched as Irene split the white dough into three equal parts. She rolled each piece back and forth with her floury hands. They looked like long snakes. Then she laid the three round strips next to each other. She pinched them together on one end.

Irene wrinkled her forehead. "Now for the tricky part." With great care she braided the strips. Over and under, over and under, just like Yaya braided her hair.

"Phew!" Irene said when she finished. "Now I have to pinch the three strips together at this other end. And the braid won't come apart. "

"Good work," Yaya said. "Time to fetch the baking paddle. It's next to the oven."

Irene would use the paddle to slide her *tsoureki* into the oven. It had a long, wooden handle so Irene would not get burnt. At the end was a flat, square metal piece to hold the bread.

Irene found the paddle and brought it inside. She reached for the flour and sprinkled it all over the flat, metal square.

"You remembered." Yaya said.

"Yes!" Irene kept sprinkling. "I don't want my *tsoureki* to stick."

"Now we must wait one more hour," Yaya said after Irene laid her *tsoureki* on the end of the paddle.

Irene folded her hands and tapped her foot. "A whole hour? Do I have to?"

"Patience," Yaya said. "The dough must rise again now that it is braided. After *that* you can bake it."

Irene eyed her loaf. "I know." She let out a breath. "That will make the loaf very light and fluffy on the inside."

"And that will please the judges," Yaya reminded her.

Just then, Irene heard a rumbling sound. Thunder? She peeked out the kitchen window. The blue sky had turned gray.

Thunder rumbled again, closer this time.

Then it began to rain.

Yaya rushed to the window. "We must bring the firewood inside. If the wood gets wet, it will not light."

Irene gasped. "Then how will I bake my bread?"

"Hurry!" Yaya cried.

Chapter 6 – Feeding Mr. Oven

Irene bolted out the kitchen door. Yaya followed. Irene scooped up one bundle of wood. Yaya picked up the other one. They ran back into the kitchen and placed them in a corner.

Irene leaned over and felt the wood. "Just in time. It's still dry."

"Thank goodness we were home," Yaya said. "Wet firewood takes a full day to dry out."

Irene walked back to the kitchen window. "I love the smell of fresh rain." She leaned over and rested her elbows on the window ledge. Then she held her chin in her hands, took a deep breath, and watched the rain fall.

Clank, clunk. Rain hopped on the chicken coop's tin roof.

Splish, splosh. Water plopped on Mr. Oven's head.

Drip, drop. Raindrops skipped on the ground. Puddles formed.

In a few minutes the rain stopped.

"The sun's out," Irene said. "And it must be very thirsty. Its rays are drinking up the puddles already."

Yaya looked outside. "Only one day of rain during the summer. It always takes us by surprise."

Soon it was four thirty. "The bread will finish rising in half an hour," Yaya stated. "Time to fire up the oven."

Irene carried a bundle of wood and followed Yaya outside. She opened the oven's metal door and laid the sticks inside. Yaya lit the wood. They waited thirty minutes. But it seemed like forever.

Finally, Yaya opened the oven door and peeked inside. "Hot enough! No need for the extra bundle of firewood you gathered. We will leave it in the kitchen."

Irene peeked inside too. "The wood has burned down. It looks like small pieces of coal."

Yaya used a long stick to shove the coals to one side. "The coals will cook the bread but must not touch it. Time for a damp rag."

Irene dashed back into the kitchen and found the rag. She took it to Yaya.

Yaya tied the rag to the end of the long stick. "Stand back." She wiped the walls and the floor of the oven with the rag.

She did not touch the coals. "Why am I doing this?" she asked.

"To clean out the ashes," Irene replied. "And the dampness makes sure the loaf's outside is crispy. But the inside will stay soft."

Yaya smiled. "You have been a good student, little pigeon."

Irene stood up tall and proud. She kissed Yaya's wrinkled cheek. "And you have been a good teacher."

Irene would become a master baker, just like Yaya. The whole village would know it. *Especially if I win the contest.*

It was finally time to feed Mr. Oven. Irene could not wait to check her loaf.

She clapped her hands. "The yeast did its job again. My *tsoureki* is double in size. It will be light and fluffy inside. Yum! I hope the judges notice how good it tastes."

Irene beat an egg with a little milk. She used a brush to coat the loaf with the mixture.

"And what will this do?" Yaya asked.

"It will give the bread a deep, golden color as it bakes," Irene answered. She sprinkled sesame seeds all over the surface. "I hope the judges notice how pretty it looks."

Irene carried the baking paddle from the kitchen.

"Careful!" Yaya called out. "Walk slowly so your *tsoureki* does not fall off."

Irene carefully crossed the yard. She slid the metal part of the paddle into the oven. Good thing the wooden handle was long! Irene felt only a little of the oven's heat.

She wiggled the handle. The *tsoureki* slid off into the oven. Irene let out a sigh of relief. Her loaf was safe inside Mr. Oven. She pulled the baking paddle out.

Yaya closed the door.

Eat up the dough, Mr. Oven, Irene thought. *Then spit out a golden loaf for me. A loaf that will win the contest!*

Irene and Yaya waited. Then they waited some more.

Irene paced around the backyard. Thirty minutes was a long time to wait for her *tsoureki* to bake!

"It's time to take the bread out," Yaya finally said.

Irene ran to the oven. What would her loaf look like? Would Mr. Oven spit out a perfect, golden loaf? Or had he turned it black?

Yaya opened the oven door.

Irene slid the metal end of the baking paddle into the oven. She carefully pushed it under the *tsoureki.* Then she pulled the paddle out. A sweet smell filled her nose.

"Mmmm!" Irene beamed. "Looks good enough to eat."

Yaya winked at Irene. "Good enough to win the contest."

"Thank you, Mr. Oven," Irene said.

She picked up the hot *tsoureki* with two kitchen towels and placed it on a glass platter.

Yaya opened the dining room door. Irene passed through and set the platter on the dining room table.

"I'll leave the dining room door open," Irene said. "My *tsoureki* will cool faster with a little breeze blowing."

They walked to the kitchen. Mama would soon need help with dinner.

Irene looked over her shoulder and smiled. Her loaf was perfect. Surely it would win the contest.

A sudden thought turned Irene's smile into a worried frown.

Has Maria baked her bread yet? And is it better than mine?

Chapter 7 – At the Table

Mama stood at the stove and fried a large fish. Irene's stomach growled. Lunch seemed a long time ago.

"You have worked hard," Mama said. "You must be hungry. Set the table. Papa is home. He's washing up."

Irene jumped to obey.

In no time, Mama put the fish, peas, and roasted potatoes on the kitchen table. She handed a round loaf of bread to

Papa. He cut slices and passed them around. Then he thanked God for the food.

Irene dug into her dinner. She took a bite of bread and remembered her *tsoureki* cooling on the dining room table. "Papa, I worked all afternoon to bake my loaf. Yaya did not help me one little bit."

"Irene did a fine job on her own," Yaya said.

Irene grinned. "You must see it, Papa. A golden crust and the smell . . ."

Papa rubbed his neck.

"You okay, Papa?" Irene asked. Her father rubbed his neck when he was worried. Surely he was not worried about her bread! "Did I not mend the nets well this morning?"

Papa smiled. "You did a good job, Irene. And your *tsoureki* sounds like a contest winner." Then he frowned. "But on the way home I ran into Mrs. Lydia."

Irene stiffened. *Did Maria tell her yaya how rude I was to her?* "And?"

"Earlier today Mrs. Lydia and Maria went to check on the family's sheep," Papa said. "They graze on the hill just outside the village. There's good grass there."

Irene's eyes got big. "Is one of the lambs hurt?"

Papa shook his head. "The sheep are fine. But Maria's firewood is not. It rained while Mrs. Lydia and Maria were on the hill."

Irene's heart sank. "They did not know it would rain when they left. Was Maria's firewood outside?"

Papa nodded. "Half a bundle was outside next to the oven. It was soaking wet by the time they made it home. The other half was inside and stayed dry."

Irene's mouth felt like cotton. She reached for her glass of water. "Poor Maria. Half a bundle of firewood might not make her oven hot enough for baking."

"Mrs. Lydia told me that Maria could have drowned the village with her tears."

Tears sprang to Irene's eyes. She looked down at her plate. She was no longer hungry.

I should have been kinder to Maria, she scolded herself. *I pray I can make it up to her—somehow!*

Chapter 8 – What Does the Good Book Say?

After dinner Yaya said, "Irene and I will clean up the dishes."

"Thank you," Mama said. She and Papa hurried out the door. They wanted to see how the setup for the Summer Festival was going.

Irene filled the sink with warm, soapy water. She soaped dishes and Yaya rinsed them.

"You are very quiet, little pigeon," Yaya said after a while. "Something on your mind?"

Irene swallowed hard. "What if Maria cannot bake her bread for the Junior Baking contest?"

"Can you do something to make sure she can?"

"No," Irene answered.

"Will it be a fair contest if Maria is not in it?"

Irene crinkled her nose. "What do you mean?"

"Everyone knows Maria is the only other girl in the village who is a good baker like you. Her yaya has taught her well."

Irene cocked her head to one side. She sighed. "I want to help Maria. I feel sorry that her wood got wet." Then she shrugged. "But that also gives me a chance to beat my enemy."

Yaya stopped rinsing plates. She looked Irene in the eyes. "What does the Good Book say?" she asked softly.

Irene looked away. She knew Yaya meant "What does the *Bible* say?" She did not want to answer. But she knew she had to.

She took a deep breath. "It says 'Love your enemies.'"

"Is Maria your enemy?"

"Yes. Because I must beat her in the contest. I *must* win."

Yaya said nothing more.

Irene's heart was heavy. It felt like the rain clouds still hung over her house.

Suddenly, she remembered her prayer at the dinner table: "*I was mean to Maria. I pray I can make it up to her— somehow!*"

Irene had an idea. It might cost her the contest. But she had to do it.

"Maria has half a bundle of dry wood," she told Yaya. "I didn't use my extra bundle of wood from the field. I will give half of it to Maria. Then she will have a full bundle. She can bake her loaf."

Yaya touched Irene's cheek. "Are you sure?"

"It is the right thing to do." Irene replied. Her heart felt light.

"It is the kind thing to do." Yaya kissed Irene's forehead. "Bless you, little pigeon."

Irene beamed. She knew the saying in Crete about a yaya's blessing: "It stays with you forever."

"We are done cleaning up," Yaya said. "It's time for me to head home. It is getting late."

"I'll see you to the front door," Irene said. "But first let me get a few radishes for Poppy."

Irene took five radishes from the fridge. She walked outside with Yaya. The setting sun cast an orange glow over the backyard.

But something did not look right. Irene's heart skipped a beat. "Yaya, Poppy is gone!"

Yaya ran to Poppy's usual place. "She chewed through her rope."

"Where could she be?" Irene looked around. Her eyes widened. "Could she have—?"

Irene bolted into the dining room. Poppy stood next to the dining room table chewing happily.

Irene looked down at her *tsoureki*.

It was half gone.

Chapter 9 – A Hard Choice

Irene's face reddened. "Bad goat!" she yelled. "Bad, bad goat. What have you done?"

Poppy stopped chewing. She stared at Irene with her round, brown eyes. Then she took another big bite of *tsoureki*.

Irene stomped her foot. "How will I enter the contest now?" She flung the radishes to the floor.

Poppy clip-clopped over to the radishes—and chomped on one. Irene marched over and stood behind the goat. "Shoo!" She shoved her out of the dining room. "And don't come back in here."

Yaya stood in the doorway. "Oh, Irene. I am so sorry."

Irene burst into tears. She covered her face with her hands. Her body shook. Her beautiful *tsoureki* was ruined. Half of it lay inside a goat's fat belly.

She cried louder.

Yaya sat down and pulled Irene onto her lap. For a long time nobody said a word. Irene sniffed as she rested her head on Yaya.

After a while, Yaya said, "Poppy has good taste."

Irene stopped sniffing. "What do you mean?"

Yaya patted Irene's hand. "Poppy could smell how tasty your *tsoureki* was. What a pity she is not a judge in the contest."

Irene thought about Poppy as a judge. Her lip twitched. Then she giggled.

Yaya took out a white hankie. She wiped Irene's cheeks. She always knew how to make Irene feel better.

"Can I still enter the contest?" Irene asked. *How will I win and make Yaya proud?*

"Tomorrow is a new day," Yaya said. "You will bake another *tsoureki*."

Irene sat up straight. "I will? Is there enough time?"

Yaya patted Irene's knee. "Plenty of time. We will start in the morning. The contest is tomorrow evening."

Irene bit her bottom lip so it would not tremble. Tears swam in her eyes. She did not want to cry again. She blinked them back. "But it is so . . . much . . . work."

"That is true," Yaya said softly. "Nothing that has value is ever easy. It comes with much work."

Irene nodded. Yaya was right. "You are the wisest yaya in the village. And in all of Crete."

Maybe in the whole world.

Irene cocked her head to one side. She thought hard. "I have enough flour and yeast for another loaf."

"And enough butter and almonds," Yaya said.

"But our chickens have not been laying many eggs."

"I will bring you two eggs from my chicken coop."

Irene let out a deep sigh. "What about wood? I have the extra bundle from the field. But I said I would give half of it to Maria. That was before I knew I would need all of it to bake another *tsoureki*. I can't gather more wood from the field. It will be too wet from the rain."

"You have a hard choice to make," Yaya said. "Maria will have a full bundle of firewood. You will be left with only half of one. Now *your* oven might not get hot enough to bake a good loaf."

Irene thought about the contest. She thought about the new earrings she wanted to buy. And she thought again about what the Good Book said.

Irene made up her mind. "I will still give half my wood to Maria. I said I would."

Just then, Mama and Papa returned. Irene joined them and tried to smile. She would be brave. "Silly Poppy ate my *tsoureki*," she said. Her voice wavered just a little.

Papa and Mama looked worried.

"I must bake another one tomorrow," Irene said.

Papa squeezed her hand. He glanced at Poppy with narrowed eyes. The goat nibbled on a tuft of grass. "Ah, that goat," he said. "Always eating. Should I send her to the butcher?"

Irene gasped. "Papa, surely you are teasing. I can make another loaf. But I cannot replace Poppy."

Papa chuckled. "Yes, I am teasing."

Irene lifted her chin. "Poppy has been a bad goat. But she has good taste. She knew my *tsoureki* would be very tasty."

Papa chuckled. "I'm sure your new loaf will be just as good."

"I hope so, Papa." Irene shrugged.

"Let the judges decide," Yaya said. Then she yawned. "Good night, everyone. See you in the morning, Irene."

"Good night. Don't forget my two eggs."

"I will have a word with my chickens," Yaya said. "They must lay two good eggs for my Irene's *tsoureki*."

Irene giggled. The chickens would never dare disobey Yaya.

Later that night Irene climbed into bed and pulled the sheets over her. They felt cool on her warm skin. She closed her eyes.

Will my new tsoureki be as good as the first one?

Irene worried about her bread until she fell asleep.

Chapter 10 – Two Answered Prayers

The next morning, the sun nudged Irene's heavy eyelids. She yawned and rubbed her eyes. *It's Friday,* she thought. She sat upright. *Finally!*

Finally, the day of the Summer Festival.

Finally, the day of the Junior Baking contest.

Then Irene remembered her wood. And Maria. She lay back down.

Her thoughts spun round and round in her head. *Should I give half my wood to Maria? What if I lose the contest? I will have to wait until next year to enter again.*

A whole year to show I am a good baker.

A whole year to make Yaya proud.

A whole year!

As Irene lay there, she decided something. It hurt, but she made up her mind once and for all. Winning a contest could wait. Making up for how mean she had been to Maria could not wait. This was the opportunity she had prayed for.

Irene jumped out of bed and got dressed. She tiptoed quietly into the kitchen. She untied the bundle of firewood, took half of it, and tied it with a string. Irene was surprised that she did not feel sad.

She quietly opened the front door and headed right. Irene turned left at the end of her street. Then she turned right again and walked halfway down. A few minutes later she stood in front of a green door.

Maria's house.

The milkman's truck stood across the street. It would make a good hiding place. But where was the milkman?

Irene looked up and down the cobbled street. She spotted the milkman at the very end. He held two bottles of milk and chatted with a woman.

Irene tiptoed to Maria's front door and set the wood down. She held her breath. Then she knocked on the door.

Run! Irene darted across the street and crouched behind the milk truck.

She thought of what Yaya always said: "Do good deeds in secret. Your Father in heaven still sees."

Irene's knees wobbled. She peeked around the side of the truck. Would Maria answer the door?

Mrs. Lydia opened the door. She looked up and down the street. Then she looked at her feet. She put a hand to her chest and gasped.

Irene kept as still as she could.

"Maria!" Mrs. Lydia called. "Come quickly."

Maria joined Mrs. Lydia. She rubbed her sleepy eyes. "What is it, Yaya?"

Mrs. Lydia pointed at their feet.

Maria's eyes widened. She bent over to touch the wood. She put her hands over her mouth and squealed. "Oh, Yaya! I prayed for dry firewood. It is a miracle." She frowned. "But do I still have time to bake my cheese bread?'

"You have time," Mrs. Lydia replied. "Let's get to work."

Irene smiled at Mrs. Lydia's words.

Maria glanced up and down the street. "Yaya, who left the wood?"

Mrs. Lydia shrugged. "I don't know. But whoever did is a good friend."

Maria nodded, picked up the wood, and paused. She looked closely at the bundle. Her eyes grew wide.

Irene's hands felt clammy. Not many walnut trees grew in the village. Did Maria see it was the same walnut wood from the field yesterday? Would she realize it came from Irene's stash?

Maria said nothing as she followed her grandmother back inside. The door closed.

Irene let out a sigh of relief. Then she ran home as fast as she could.

Time to bake another sweet, tasty *tsoureki!*

CHAPTER 11 – Mr. Oven Gets Fired Up Again

Yaya waited in the kitchen. She did not ask where Irene had been. But Irene was sure Yaya knew. Yaya had a way of knowing everything.

"Good morning," Irene said. "Thanks for coming to help again."

"We have much to do," Yaya said. "But first a good breakfast. For strength."

"Where are Papa and Mama?" asked Irene.

"Papa went fishing," Yaya replied. "Mama went to the store to buy a nice, thick rope. To tie up Poppy."

Irene chuckled. "Good. Poppy will not escape again."

Yaya put two plates, sausages, olives, and sliced tomatoes on the table. She cut a slice of round bread. Irene spread a thick layer of butter on her slice. Then Yaya poured two glasses of chilled goat's milk.

"At least Poppy is good for one thing," Yaya said as she took a sip. "She makes good milk." She took out a jar of jam from her purse.

Maria's face beamed. "Your homemade blackberry jam. My favorite. Thank you, Yaya."

"Sweet things for sweet girls," Yaya said.

After breakfast Irene got to work making another *tsoureki.* She stirred the mixture. She kneaded the dough and let it rise. She braided the three long pieces. Her arms ached worse than they did yesterday. She let the dough rise again.

Irene used every stick of firewood she had left. She paced up and down by the oven while the wood burned. "Will it be hot enough?" she asked Yaya.

Yaya peeked into the oven. "Hot enough to cook your bread. But we will see if the loaf rises well."

"Or if it browns well," Irene added.

The oven was finally ready for baking. Irene brushed the egg and milk mixture on the loaf. She sprinkled it with sesame seeds. She eased it onto the wooden baking paddle. Then she carefully slid the *tsoureki* into the oven's mouth.

Eat up, Mr. Oven.

At noon it was time to take the bread out. "Spit me out a *tsoureki* that will win the contest, Mr. Oven," Irene said. She pulled the bread out with the baking paddle.

Her heart sank.

"Oh, Yaya. The *tsoureki* has risen only a little. And it is only light brown."

Tears sprang to her eyes. *There is no way I can win now.*

Yaya looked at the loaf. "It is not *that* bad, little pigeon. The judges will taste it. You still have a chance."

"It's not as good as yesterday's loaf." Irene blinked back her tears. "But I did the best I could with half a bundle of wood."

Maria really is a kind girl, Irene thought. *I will be okay if she wins. Maybe we can even be friends.*

Chapter 12 – Getting Ready

Soon the family sat down to lunch in the kitchen. The *tsoureki* cooled in the dining room. Now and then Irene glanced nervously out the window. She hoped Poppy would behave this time.

"You have hardly touched your food, Irene," Mama said.

"Poppy will not chew through her new rope," Papa said. "It is too thick."

Yaya patted Irene's hand. "Think of how fun the Summer Festival will be tonight."

Irene's face brightened. "What games will they have this year? Will there be new rides?"

"This morning I saw people setting up," Mama said.

"I saw them too," Papa said. "The churchyard is crammed with tables and tents and boxes."

Irene clapped her hands. "I can't wait! Did you see Mikhali the jeweler?"

Papa nodded.

"Yay! He makes beautiful earrings. I will buy a new pair." She sighed. "If I win."

That afternoon the sun threw a thick, yellow blanket over the village. Irene yawned.

"We will stay up very late tonight at the festival," Mama said. "Lie down and rest for a while."

Irene crossed her arms. "Do I have to?"

"Join me for a nap," Yaya said.

Irene didn't want to sleep. But she wanted to cuddle with Yaya. So she agreed.

They both lay down in Irene's bedroom.

A few minutes passed. Irene could hear Yaya's gentle snoring. She snuggled up to her. Yaya stirred but did not wake up.

Irene shut her eyes tight. But sleep would not come. Her thoughts twirled. Maria. The *tsoureki*. The festival. And . . . the contest. It seemed like forever before tonight would come. Like time itself had gone to sleep.

Finally, the shadows outside grew longer. The day turned cooler.

Surely we can get up now! Irene nudged Yaya. "It's time to get ready for the Summer Festival."

Yaya yawned.

Irene jumped out of bed and skipped to the closet. "I'll wear my new green dress. The one you sewed for me. Just for the contest. I love the white daisies around the hem." She wriggled into her dress.

Irene combed out her dark, tight curls. They bounced right back up. Then she watched Yaya get ready.

Yaya always wore black since *Papou*, Irene's grandfather, had died. But on special occasions she wore navy blue. Yaya tucked loose strands of gray hair under her navy scarf. She put a clean, white hankie in her navy apron pocket. Her brown shoes shone.

"You are the prettiest yaya in the village," Irene said.

Yaya laughed. Her green eyes sparkled. "And you are the prettiest little pigeon in all of Crete."

Irene touched Yaya's right cheek. "Your cheek dimples just like mine does when *I* laugh."

Yaya kissed Irene's fingers. "Come along. It's almost time to go."

At six o'clock, Irene and Yaya strolled arm in arm toward the village church. Papa wore his new white shirt. Mama wore her new yellow dress. She carried Irene's *tsoureki* on a silver platter.

"I hear music and talking and laughter," Irene said. "I want to enjoy every minute of tonight. I hope time slows down, Yaya."

"I hope so too." Yaya squeezed Irene's arm. "But time has a way of flying away much too fast."

"Look!" Irene cried. "I can see the top of the church. Round light bulbs are lighting up the churchyard. Come on! Let's walk faster."

Irene let go of Yaya's arm and skipped ahead down the road. Two rows of tall pine trees lined the pathway to the church.

"We're here," Irene shouted. "Finally! The Summer Festival."

Chapter 13 - The Summer Festival

Yaya, Irene, Mama, and Papa entered the churchyard.

Mama raised her voice above the noise. "Papa and I will take your loaf to the judges."

"Thank you," Irene called as her parents walked away. She turned to Yaya and pointed to a nearby stand. "I'm going to play the duck game. I'll catch up with you later."

Irene skipped away. At the duck game stand she threw ten large, plastic rings at a row of moving ducks. Eight of them landed around a duck's neck. The stand owner handed her a pink bracelet. Irene proudly put on her prize.

After that Irene headed to Mikhali the jeweler's stand. She looked through the earrings. One pair sparkled. Dangly, silver earrings with a green stone in the middle. *These would look great with my new green dress.*

A tap on her shoulder broke into Irene's thoughts. She spun around.

Maria was smiling at her. "Nice to see you again, Irene."

Irene's heart leaped up. "H-hello"

"I like those earrings," Maria said. "The green stone matches your eyes. And your dress. Will you buy them?"

"I was going to buy them with the prize . . ." Irene's voice trailed off.

Maria stopped smiling. She twirled a lock of sandy brown hair. "I hope you win the contest. Then you can buy the earrings."

Irene's heart fluttered. Did Maria really mean that?

I think she does! She squeezed Maria's hand. "Thanks. I also wish you well in the contest." *I really mean it too!* Her heart filled with joy.

"Thanks." Maria bit her lip. She looked at her feet. Then she took a deep breath. "Irene, thank you for the—"

"Maria!"

The girls turned around. Mrs. Lydia waved for Maria to join her at the popcorn stand.

"I have to go." Maria hugged Irene and left.

Irene frowned. *Was Maria about to thank me for the wood? Now I will never know.*

Irene strolled through the rows of tables and stands and small tents. She wanted to keep her mind off the contest. And off Maria.

Little girls pulled on their mothers' skirts and pointed to cotton candy. A group of women gathered around a kitchen goods stand. They dug through piles of blue and yellow and orange table cloths.

Little boys pulled on their fathers' trousers and pointed to carnival rides. A group of men gathered around a stand with fishermen's supplies. They picked up fishing hooks and studied them.

Irene saw Papa among the men. She waved. He smiled and waved back.

Irene spotted Yaya buying yarn and joined her. "How about some candied nuts?" Yaya asked.

"Oh, yes please! I can smell them from here."

Yaya and Irene strolled down a row of stands. At the end of the row, a young man sat on a chair. He played a mandolin. People threw coins into an upturned hat in front of him.

Irene stopped. Eyes wide, she watched the young man's hands. They flew up and down the mandolin's neck.

What a funny-looking instrument, Irene thought. *Looks like half a pear.* She tapped her foot on the ground. The mandolin made a lovely sound. Like a thousand, trembling, small bells.

"You're enjoying the music," Yaya said. "Would you like to learn to play the mandolin?"

Irene nodded. "Maria offered to teach me how to play."

Yaya raised an eyebrow. "She did?"

Irene hung her head. "But I was so rude to her yesterday. I'm sure she's changed her mind." What would Yaya say about that?

She didn't say anything. A loud message blared over the loudspeakers instead. "Time for the results of the Junior Baking contest. Please come to the main stage area."

Irene's heart pounded. *Time for the results.* The words raced through her mind. Her arms felt floppy.

Time for the results.

Her legs felt like the jellyfish she often saw bobbing up and down in the sea.

Time for the results.

Yaya put an arm around Irene's shoulder. "We'll buy the candied nuts later. Come on. Let's find out who won the contest."

Chapter 14 – And the Winner Is . . .

Yaya and Irene made their way to the main stage area. A crowd had already gathered. Papa and Mama stood near the front. They waved Irene and Yaya over.

A tall microphone stood at the center of the stage. Mr. Panos, the mayor, strode up to the microphone. He tapped it with his finger. Then he cleared his throat.

"Good evening, everyone. I have the results of the Junior Baking contest. It was a close contest this year. First place wins 500 drachmas. Second place wins a blue ribbon. Third place wins a white ribbon."

The crowd became very quiet.

"I will now announce first, second, and third place winners. Please join me on the stage when I call your name."

Irene's knees wobbled. Her head spun. She clutched Yaya's hand. *Please, please, please!*

Mr. Panos cleared his throat again. He looked at a piece of paper in his hand. "First place goes to . . . Maria Raptis for her cheese bread!"

Irene's heart fell to her stomach in a big lump. She watched Maria walk up on the stage.

Maria's face was flushed. She shook the mayor's hand. He handed her an envelope.

Yaya squeezed Irene's hand. "You did your best, little pigeon."

Irene blinked back tears. "It hurts. But I know I did the right thing, Yaya. It's okay I didn't win."

Irene ducked her head and started to walk away.

"Second place goes to Irene Stavros for her *tsoureki*," the mayor announced.

Irene gasped. *What?* Her head snapped up. She stared at Yaya. "Did I hear right?"

Yaya nodded.

Second place! She didn't win. But second place was not so bad. It actually felt pretty good.

"Well done!" Yaya cried. She nudged Irene toward the stage.

"I hope I don't faint," Irene mumbled.

She walked onto the stage. Her cheeks warmed. She shook the mayor's hand. He pinned a blue ribbon on her dress. "Congratulations, Irene."

Everyone clapped.

Irene left the stage and joined Yaya, Papa, and Mama. They hugged and kissed her. When the mayor called out third place, they clapped for the winner.

Maria came up afterward and shook Irene's hand. "Well done."

Irene touched her blue ribbon. She smiled at Maria. "Well done too, Maria. I'm sure your cheese bread was great." She paused. "Can you stay?"

Irene wanted to sit and visit with Maria. She had so many questions.

How did you make your bread?

Do you like looking after sheep? How many do you have?

What are your favorite toys?

How long did it take you to learn to play the mandolin?

Maria shook her head. "I'm sorry, but I can't stay. I have to go."

Irene's face fell. "Oh."

"We have to be up early to take the sheep to graze."

"I understand." Irene nodded. "Good bye."

"Good bye."

Irene watched Maria walk away. Tears welled up. *I didn't win the contest. But even worse . . . I didn't make Maria my friend.*

Chapter 15 - Sweet Friendship

The next morning Irene woke up late. She picked up her blue ribbon and gazed at it. She had slept with it on her pillow.

After breakfast Irene helped Mama clean the house. They dusted and swept and mopped.

Yaya came for a visit that afternoon. "Time for tea." She held up a little packet of green leaves.

Irene licked her lips. She liked tea a little. But they always ate round butter cookies with tea. Irene liked Yaya's butter cookies a *lot*.

Yaya boiled water on the stove. She added the tea leaves. "I picked them myself this morning from the nearby hill," she said. "Get the honey, Irene."

Mama, Yaya, and Irene sat outside under the blackberry tree. Irene sipped her tea. It was sweet and tasted like flowers and the earth mixed together. She let a bite of butter cookie melt in her mouth.

Tap, tap, tap. A knock sounded at the front door.

Mama's eyebrows went up. "We are not expecting company." She headed to answer the front door.

Irene heard Mrs. Lydia's voice. Then she heard footsteps.

Mama came outside with Mrs. Lydia and—

"Maria!" Irene grinned.

Mama nodded to two empty chairs around the table. "Please join us for tea."

"Thank you." Mrs. Lydia sat down. "Maria wanted . . . well, *we* wanted to come visit."

Maria looked at her feet and played with a lock of hair. She chewed on her lower lip.

"Sit next to me, Maria." Irene patted the empty chair.

The corners of Maria's mouth jumped up. She sat down next to Irene.

"Wasn't that a wonderful Summer Festival last night?" Mama said.

"Just lovely," Mrs. Lydia replied. "I was sad we couldn't stay longer."

Irene sipped her tea. It made her nervous tummy feel better. She listened to the women talk. Now and then she smiled at Maria.

"Irene," Mama said after a few minutes. "Maybe Maria would like to meet Poppy."

Maria nodded eagerly. "Oh, yes, I would."

Irene fetched a handful of radishes and led Maria over to her goat.

Maria petted Poppy's head. Poppy nibbled Maria's dress.

"Silly goat," Irene scolded. "Here are some radishes. Do not eat my friend's dress."   Maria's face beamed.

"Would you like to play a game?" Irene asked. "Or we can dress my dolls."

"Let's do both," Maria answered. "Oh, and perhaps next time you and your yaya can come to my house. I'd love to teach you to play the mandolin."

Irene giggled. *It looks like Maria will be my friend, after all.*

Later that night Yaya picked up her purse and got ready to leave. "I'll see you in church tomorrow, Irene."

"Yaya . . ." Irene had a question but was not sure how to ask it. "Are you . . .?" She paused.

Yaya sat down. "What is it, little pigeon?"

Irene thought hard. But the words would still not come out.

Yaya patted Irene's hand. "Am I upset with you?"

Irene nodded.

Yaya shook her head. "No! I am proud of you. Very proud."

Irene let out a sigh of relief. "But I didn't win."

"To me, you *are* a winner."

Irene wrinkled her eyebrows. "What do you mean, Yaya?"

"You learned a very important lesson," Yaya replied. "More important than baking the best bread."

Irene felt a lump in her throat. She swallowed hard. "I'm not sure I understand."

"We have a saying in our village," Yaya said. "'An enemy cannot become a friend.'"

Irene nodded. She knew that saying well.

Yaya sighed. "It's not true. That is not what the Good Book says. We were once all enemies of God. But through Jesus He has made us His friends."

"Yes," Irene said softly.

"And you, Irene, learned this lesson," Yaya went on. "An enemy *can* be made into a friend. You just needed to open your heart."

Irene eyes filled with tears. She threw her arms around Yaya.

At the front door Yaya reached into her purse. "I almost forgot. Mrs. Lydia gave this to me earlier today. When she and Maria came for tea. It is a gift from Maria to you." Yaya handed Irene a small packet wrapped in brown paper.

Irene's heart pounded as she opened the package. She gasped. "The earrings I wanted from Mikhali the jeweler. Silver with a green stone. Oh, Yaya! Maria used her prize money to buy me a gift."

Yaya helped Irene put them on and kissed her forehead. "Good-night, little pigeon. You look lovely in those new earrings."

Irene kissed Yaya good-night. She watched her grandmother stroll down the street. Yaya turned and waved to Irene.

Irene waved back. Then she closed the door and leaned against it. She thought of all the good things in her life:

How blessed I am that God can be my friend.
How blessed I am to have such a wise Yaya.
And how blessed I am to have a new friend . . . Maria.

A study guide for *Irene and the Baking Contest* is available on effiehill.com

About the Author

Effie Damianidou Hill is originally from the island of Cyprus but grew up in South Africa. Effie holds a graduate degree in French literature and previously taught French at the college level. She lived in France for several years and has traveled extensively. A Chicago suburb is currently her home where she lives with her husband and homeschools their three children. She loves ancient Greek history and seeks to make learning fun by writing educational but humorous books for children. She is a certified minister and also holds a Masters Degree in Theological Studies. You can contact Effie at: effiehill@gmail.com.

Printed in Great Britain
by Amazon

18326776R00037